WALT DISNEY'S

Peter Pan

FROM THE MOTION PICTURE "PETER PAN"

BASED ON THE STORY BY
SIR JAMES M. BARRIE

ILLUSTRATIONS BY THE WALT DISNEY STUDIO

PICTURES ADAPTED BY JOHN HENCH
AND AL DEMPSTER

SKULL ROCK

CROCODILE CREEK

MERMAID LAGOON

A GOLDEN BOOK • NEW YORK
Western Publishing Company, Inc.,
Racine, Wisconsin 53404

I N A quiet street in London lived the Darling family. There were Father and Mother Darling, and Wendy, Michael, and John. There was also the children's nursemaid, Nana—a St. Bernard dog.

For Nana and the children the best hour of the day was bedtime, for then they were together in the nursery. There Wendy told wonderful stories about Peter Pan of Never Land. This Never Land was a magical spot with Indians and Mermaids and Fairies—and wicked pirates, too.

John and Michael liked best of all to play pirate. They had some fine, slashing duels between Peter Pan and his arch-enemy, the Pirate Captain Hook.

Father Darling did not like this kind of play. He blamed it on Wendy's stories of Peter Pan, and Father Darling did not approve of those stories, either.

"It is time for Wendy to grow up," he decided. "This is your last night in the nursery, Wendy girl."

All the children were much upset at that. Without Wendy in the nursery there would be no more stories of Peter Pan! Then to make matters worse, Father Darling became annoyed with Nana and decided the children were too old to be treated like puppies. So he tied Nana in the garden for the night.

When Mother and Father Darling had gone out for the evening, leaving the children snug in their beds with Nana on guard, below, who should come to the nursery but Peter Pan! It seemed he had been flying in from Never Land to listen to the bedtime stories, all unseen. Only Nana had caught sight of him once and nipped off his shadow as he escaped. So back he came, looking for his lost shadow and hoping for a

story about himself. With him was a fairy, Tinker Bell. When Peter heard that Wendy was to be moved from the nursery, he hit upon a plan. "I'll take you to Never Land with me, to tell stories to my Lost Boys!" he decided as Wendy sewed his shadow back on.

Wendy thought that was a lovely idea—if Michael and John could go, too. So Peter Pan taught them all to fly—with happy thoughts and faith and trust, and a sprinkling of Tinker Bell's pixie dust. Then out the nursery window they sailed, heading for Never Land, while Nana barked frantically below.

Back in Never Land, on the pirate ship, Captain Hook was as usual grumbling about Peter Pan. You see, once in a fair fight long ago Peter Pan had cut off one of the pirate captain's hands, so that he had to wear a hook instead. Then Pan threw the hand to a crocodile, who enjoyed the taste of Hook so much that he had been lurking around ever since hoping to nibble at the rest of him. Fortunately for the pirate, the crocodile had also swallowed a clock. He went "tick tock" when he came near, which gave a warning to Captain Hook.

Now, as Captain Hook grumbled about his young enemy, there was a call from the crow's nest.

"Peter Pan ahoy!"

"What? Where?" shouted Hook, twirling his spy-glass around the sky. And then he spied Peter and the children, pausing for a rest on a cloud. "Swoggle me eyes, it *is* Pan!" Hook gloated. "Pipe up the crew. . . . Man the guns. . . . We'll get him this time at last!"

"Oh, Peter, it's just as I've dreamed it would be—Mermaid Lagoon and all," Wendy was saying when the first of the pirates' cannonballs ripped through the cloud close beside their feet and went sizzling on past.

"Look out!" cried Pan. "Tinker Bell, take Wendy and the boys to the island. I'll stay here and draw Hook's fire!"

Away flew Tinker Bell, as fast as she could go. In her naughty little heart she hoped the children would fall behind and be lost. Especially was she jealous of the Wendy girl who seemed to have won Peter Pan's heart.

Straight through the Never Land jungle Tink flew, down into a clearing beside an old dead tree called Hangman's Tree. She landed on a toadstool, bounced to a shiny leaf, and pop! a secret door opened for her in the knot of the hollow tree.

Zip! Down a slippery tunnel Tink slid. She landed at the bottom in an underground room—the secret house of Peter Pan.

Ting-a-ling! she tinkled, flitting about from one corner of the room to the next. She was trying to awaken the sleeping Lost Boys, who lay like so many curled-up balls of fur.

At last, rather grumpily, they woke up and stretched in their little fur suits. And they listened to Tinker Bell.

"What? Pan wants us to shoot down a terrible Wendy bird? Lead us to it!" they shouted, and out they hurried.

When Wendy and Michael and John appeared, flying wearily, the Lost Boys tried to pelt them with stones and sticks—especially the "Wendy bird." Down tumbled Wendy, all her happy thoughts destroyed —for without them no one can fly.

"Hurray! We got the Wendy bird!" the Lost Boys shouted.

But then Peter Pan arrived. How angry he was when he discovered that the boys had tried to shoot down Wendy, even though he had caught her before she could be hurt.

"I brought her to be a mother to us all and to tell us stories," he said.

"Come on, Wendy," said Peter. "I'll show you the Mermaids. Boys, take Michael and John to hunt some Indians."

So Peter and Wendy flew away, and the boys marched off through the forest, planning to capture some Indians. There were wild animals all around, but the boys never thought to be afraid, and not a creature harmed them as through the woods they went.

"First we'll surround the Indians," John decided. "Then we'll take them by surprise."

John's plan worked splendidly, but it was the Indians who used it. Disguised as moving trees, they quietly surrounded the boys and took *them* by surprise!

Soon, bound with ropes, the row of boys marched away, led by the Indians to their village on the cliff.

"Don't worry, the Indians are our friends," the Lost Boys said, but the chief looked stern.

Meanwhile, on the other side of the island, Wendy and Peter were visiting the Mermaids in their peaceful Mermaid Lagoon. As they were chatting together, Peter suddenly said, "Hush!"

A boat from the pirate ship was going by. In it were wicked Captain Hook and Smee, the pirate cook. And at the stern, all bound with ropes, sat Princess Tiger Lily, daughter of the Indian chief.

"We'll make her talk," sneered Captain Hook.

"She'll tell us where Peter Pan lives, or we'll leave her tied to slippery Skull Rock, where the tide will wash over her."

But proud and loyal Tiger Lily would not say a single word.

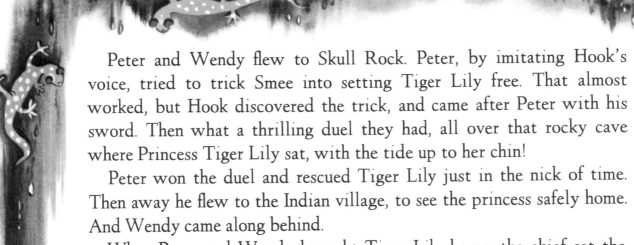

Peter and Wendy flew to Skull Rock. Peter, by imitating Hook's voice, tried to trick Smee into setting Tiger Lily free. That almost worked, but Hook discovered the trick, and came after Peter with his sword. Then what a thrilling duel they had, all over that rocky cave where Princess Tiger Lily sat, with the tide up to her chin!

Peter won the duel and rescued Tiger Lily just in the nick of time. Then away he flew to the Indian village, to see the princess safely home. And Wendy came along behind.

When Peter and Wendy brought Tiger Lily home, the chief set the captives all free. Then what a wonderful feast they had! All the boys did Indian dances and learned wild Indian chants, and Peter Pan was made a chief! Only Wendy had no fun at all, for she had to help the squaws carry firewood.

"I've had enough of Never Land," she thought grumpily. "I'm ready to go home right now!"

While the Indian celebration was at its height, Smee the pirate crept up through the underbrush and captured Tinker Bell.

Trapped in his cap, she struggled and kicked, but Smee took her back to the pirate ship and presented her to Captain Hook.

"Ah, Miss Bell," said Hook sympathetically, "I've heard how badly Peter Pan has treated you since that scheming girl Wendy came. How nice it would be if we could kidnap her and take her off to sea to scrub the decks and cook for the pirate crew!"

Tink tinkled happily at the thought.

"But, alas," sighed Hook, "we don't know where Pan's house is, so we cannot get rid of Wendy for you."

Tink thought this over. "You won't hurt Peter?" she asked, in solemn tinkling tones. "Of course not!" promised Hook.

Then she marched to a map of Never Land and traced a path to Peter's hidden house.

"Thank you, my dear," said wicked Captain Hook, and he locked her up in a lantern cage, while he went off to capture Peter Pan!

MOUNTAINS   BOG   HANGMAN'S TREE

That night when Wendy tucked the children into their beds in the underground house, she talked to them about home and mother. Soon they were all so homesick that they wanted to leave at once for home. Wendy invited all the Lost Boys to come and live with the Darling family. Only Peter refused to go. He simply looked the other way as Wendy and the boys told him good-by and climbed the tunnel to Hangman's Tree.

Up in the woods near Hangman's Tree waited Hook and his pirate band. As each boy came out, a hand was clapped over his mouth and he was quickly tied up with ropes. Last of all came Wendy. Zip, zip, she was bound up too, and the crew marched off with their load of children, back to the pirate ship.

"Blast it!" muttered Hook. "We still don't have Pan!"

So he and Smee left a wicked bomb, wrapped as a gift from Wendy, for poor Peter to find. Very soon, they hoped, Peter would open it and blow himself straight out of Never Land.

Imagine how terrible Tinker Bell felt when she saw all the children prisoners, and knew it was her fault!

The boys were given the terrible choice between turning pirates and walking the plank. To the boys the life of a pirate sounded fine, sad to say, and they were all ready to join up. But Wendy was shocked at that. "Never!" she cried.

"Very well," said Hook. "Then you shall be the first to walk the plank, my dear."

Everyone felt so terrible—though Wendy was ever so brave—that no one noticed when Tinker Bell escaped and flew off to warn Peter Pan.

What a dreadful moment when Wendy said good-by and bravely walked out the long narrow plank.

And then she disappeared. Everyone listened, breathless, waiting for a splash, but not a sign of one came! What could the silence mean?

Then they heard a familiar, happy crow. It was Pan in the rigging, high above. Warned by Tinker Bell, he had escaped just in time to scoop up Wendy in mid-air and fly with her to safety.

"This time you have gone too far, Hook," Peter cried.

He swooped down from the rigging, all set for a duel. And what a duel it was!

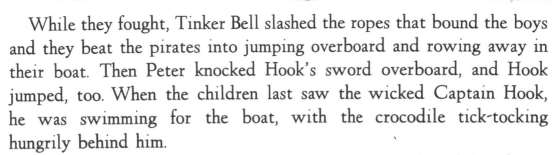

While they fought, Tinker Bell slashed the ropes that bound the boys and they beat the pirates into jumping overboard and rowing away in their boat. Then Peter knocked Hook's sword overboard, and Hook jumped, too. When the children last saw the wicked Captain Hook, he was swimming for the boat, with the crocodile tick-tocking hungrily behind him.

Peter Pan took command of the pirate ship. "Heave those halyards. Up with the jib. We're sailing to London," he cried.

"Oh, Michael! John!" cried Wendy. "We're going home!"

And sure enough, with happy thoughts and faith and trust, and a liberal sprinkling of pixie dust, away flew that pirate ship through the skies till the gangplank was run out to the Darlings' nursery windowsill.

But now that they had arrived, the Lost Boys did not want to stay. "We've sort of decided to stick with Pan," they said.

So Wendy, John, and Michael waved good-by as Peter Pan's ship sailed off through the sky, taking the Lost Boys home to Never Land, where they still live today.